AMANDA PIG
ON
HER OWN

Jean Van Leeuwen
PICTURES BY
ANN SCHWENINGER

PUFFIN BOOKS

To Elizabeth
now and always, my sweet potato
J.V.L.

For my mother Alice
A.S.

PUFFIN BOOKS
Published by the Penguin Group
Penguin Putnam Books for Young Readers,
345 Hudson Street, New York, New York 10014, U.S.A.
Penguin Books Ltd, 80 Strand, London WC2R ORL, England
Penguin Books Australia Ltd, 250 Camberwell Road, Camberwell, Victoria 3124, Australia
Penguin Books Canada Ltd, 10 Alcorn Avenue, Toronto, Ontario, Canada M4V 3B2
Penguin Books (N.Z.) Ltd, 182-190 Wairau Road, Auckland 10, New Zealand

Penguin Books Ltd, Registered Offices: Harmondsworth, Middlesex, England

First published in the United States of America by Dial Books for Young Readers,
a division of Penguin Books USA, Inc., 1991
First published by Puffin Books, a division of Penguin Putnam Books for Young Readers, 1994

19   20   18

Text copyright © Jean Van Leeuwen, 1991
Illustrations copyright © Ann Schweninger, 1991
All rights reserved

LIBRARY OF CONGRESS CATALOGING-IN-PUBLICATION DATA
Van Leeuwen, Jean.
Amanda Pig on Her Own / Jean Van Leeuwen ; pictures by Ann Schweninger.
p.   cm.—(Puffin easy-to-read)
"Reading level 2.1"—T.p. verso.
Summary: When her brother goes off to school, Amanda finds new things to do,
including ballet dancing, cleaning her room, and making a very sad,
mad day go away, with the help of mother hugs from Mother Pig.
ISBN 0-14-037144-3
[1. Pigs—Fiction.   2. Self-reliance—Fiction.]   I. Schweninger, Ann, ill. II. Title. III. Series.
PZ7.V3273Ao 1994   [E]—dc20   94-16920   CIP   AC
Puffin® and Easy-to-Read® are registered trademarks of Penguin Putnam Inc.

Printed in the United States of America

Reading Level 2.1

CONTENTS

WITHOUT OLIVER

"Good-bye, Amanda," said Oliver.

"Too bad you are too little

to go to school."

Oliver climbed on the school bus.

Mother and Father and Amanda waved.

The bus drove away.

And there was Amanda,

left at home without Oliver.

"I am not too little to go to school,"

said Amanda.

"See. I am as tall as the table."

"Why so you are," said Mother.

"You may be big enough for school

but you are not old enough yet.

Next year you will go to school."

Without Oliver the house seemed quiet.

"What shall we do together today?"

asked Amanda.

'Right now I am doing the washing,"

said Mother. "And then the ironing.

Later we can do something together."

Amanda went to her room.

She set her little table

and cooked breakfast for her animals.

But it was no fun without Oliver.

She put together her circus puzzle.

But it was no fun without Oliver.

Then she went outside and played
Mighty Pig and the Amazing Baby Pig
Meet the Bad Guys.

But without Oliver to tie up
the bad guys and take them to jail,
it was no fun at all.

Amanda went back inside.

"I am all alone," she said.

"There is nothing to do without Oliver."

"You are never all alone," said Mother.

"You always have yourself."

"I do?" said Amanda.

"Yes," said Mother.

"With Oliver you do lots of things
that you both like to do.
But without him you can do things
that just *you* like to do."
Amanda went back to her room.
She thought about things
that she liked to do.
She liked to dance. Oliver hated it.

"I will practice ballet," she said.

Amanda went to the dress-up box.

Out of Father's long underwear

and flowers from Mother's hat

and an old lace tablecloth

she made a ballet costume.

"Now," she said,

"I am the Sugar Plum Fairy."

Amanda jumped and whirled and twirled

all around the room.

Mother peeked in the door.

"I am ready to do something together,"

she said.

"I am doing what *I* like to do,"

said Amanda. "I am dancing."

"Oh, I love to dance," said Mother.

"May I join you?"

"Certainly," said Amanda.

And the two of them

jumped and whirled and twirled

all around the room

without Oliver.

SICK IN BED

"*Achoo!*" said Amanda.

"Mother, please come here. I am sick."

Mother came.

"What is wrong?" she asked.

"My nose is all stuffed up,"
said Amanda.

"Poor Amanda," said Mother.

"You must be getting a cold.

I think you should stay in bed."

She brought Amanda tissues

and books to read

and tucked her in nice and warm.

"Rest, my sweet potato," Mother said.

"Soon you will feel better."

"Mother!" called Amanda. "Come here."

Mother came.

"Now I am coughing too," said Amanda.

"Would you like to hear?"

Amanda coughed for Mother.

"Poor Amanda," said Mother.

She brought her juice

and paper to draw pictures on.

"Keep resting," she said.

"Mother!" called Amanda. "Come here."

Mother came.

"I sneezed three times," said Amanda.

"And now my nose is hot

and my eyes are all juicy."

"Poor Amanda," said Mother.

"I am very poor," said Amanda.

"And poor Sallie Rabbit," said Mother.

"She doesn't look well at all.

I'm afraid you have given her your cold."

"I think you are right," said Amanda.

"I just heard her sneeze."

"Oh dear," said Mother.

"Who is going to take care of her?"

"I will," said Amanda.

"I am her mother, you know."

Mother brought more tissues
and more juice and more books.
"I need my doctor kit too,"
said Amanda. "And my cooking things.
And maybe a few games."

Amanda tucked Sallie in nice and warm.
"Rest, my sweet potato," she said.
"Soon you will feel better."

When Mother came back a little later,

Amanda and Sallie were reading

and playing checkers

and something was cooking on the stove.

"How are my two sick ones?" she asked.

"Well," said Amanda,

"Sallie sneezed twelve times

and coughed eleven

and she has a very bad temperature.

But I am making some nice hot soup.

That will make her better."

"And how are you?" asked Mother.

"Oh, I am all better," said Amanda.

"So soon?" said Mother.

"I have to be," said Amanda.

"I am her mother, you know."

THE BIG MESS

Mother was always saying,

"Hang up your clothes, Amanda."

Father was always saying,

"Put away your toys, Amanda."

Amanda was tired of it.

"I like my clothes and toys
on the floor," she said.

"That way I can see what I have.
And I am always ready to play."

"But your room is a big mess,"
said Mother.

"I like a big mess," said Amanda.

"Well," said Father. "It is your room."

"If you want a big mess,
you can have one," said Mother.

Every day Amanda read books
and dressed up and built with blocks
and cooked for her animals.
And she never put anything away.

26

When she took off her clothes,

she dropped them wherever she was.

The big mess got bigger.

One day Mother and Amanda

were going to the store.

"I can't find my flower shirt,"

said Amanda.

"Wear your frog one," said Mother.

Amanda could not find her frog shorts.

She looked under the bed.

"Achoo!" she said. "It's dusty here."

"It's always dusty in a big mess,"
said Mother.

Amanda had to wear her frog shirt
and her flower shorts.

The next day after school

Amanda and Oliver were playing games.

"Uh-oh," said Amanda.

"Two of my checkers are missing."

"We can play dominoes," said Oliver.

But six dominoes were missing.

"Look in that pile," said Amanda.

Oliver waded into the pile.

"Uh-oh!" he said.

"You broke my teapot," said Amanda.

"I couldn't help it," said Oliver.

"You can't tell what

you are stepping on in this big mess."

The big mess got even bigger.

Amanda wore her frog shirt

with her snow pants

and her flower shorts

with her pajama top.

All her games had pieces missing.

And she was sneezing all the time.

One day Father said,

"Let's go on a picnic."

"Hooray!" cried Oliver and Amanda.

But Amanda could not find her sundress

or her ball or her jump rope.

Even Sallie Rabbit was missing.

Amanda went to tell Mother.

But she tripped over her marbles

and fell down.

"Help!" she called.

Mother and Father came running.

"Where are you?" they asked.

"Under all this stuff,"

said a tiny voice.

Mother and Father dug her out.

"Sometimes this happens

with a big mess," said Father.

"We are all ready to go," said Mother.

"Wait," said Amanda.

And she started cleaning up.

Soon she found her sundress and her ball.

And her jump rope and Sallie Rabbit.

"I am ready to go too," she said.

"Amazing," said Father.

"What happened to your big mess?"

"I like a big mess," said Amanda.

"But sometimes it is a bother."

THE BAD SAD MAD DAY

It was raining.

And there were eggs for breakfast.

Amanda looked out the window

and down at her plate

and she didn't know which was worse.

Father left the table.

Oliver left the table.

Amanda left the table.

"Where are you going?" asked Mother.

"I don't want my egg," said Amanda.

"Sit down, young lady," said Mother.

Amanda looked at her egg a long time.

Then she held her nose and ate it.

Father left the house.

Oliver left the house.

"I want to go somewhere," said Amanda.

"Not on such a rainy day," said Mother.

"Will you paint a picture for me?"

"I don't want to," said Amanda.

But she got out her paints.

She painted a picture of the rain,

all in purple.

"Purple is my favorite color," she said.

"I wish my room was purple."

She tried some purple paint on her wall.

It looked so nice that she painted

a great big purple rain cloud.

"Amanda!" said Mother.

"Paint goes on paper, not on walls."

"I like painting walls," said Amanda.

But Mother made her scrub her wall

until it was clean again.

For lunch Mother made tomato soup.

"I'd rather have peanut butter,"

said Amanda.

"You don't seem very happy today,"

said Mother.

"I am not," said Amanda.

"I am having a sad day."

After lunch Amanda built a skyscraper.

But it fell down.

Then she dressed up like a fancy lady.

But Mother said,

"Is that my lipstick you are using?"

"It is a sad mad day," said Amanda.

She went into the living room

and started to dance.

Around and around she whirled,

up on the couch,

over the big chair,

and into a table.

Crash! The lamp toppled over.

"That was my best lamp," said Mother.

"I don't care!" Amanda yelled.

"I don't care! I don't care!"

"Well I do!" Mother yelled back.

Then suddenly she stopped.

She picked up Amanda

and carried her to the big chair

and hugged her.

"Why are you doing that?" Amanda asked.

"Because you are feeling bad,"

said Mother.

"This is the best way I know to help."

"I am feeling bad and sad and mad,"

said Amanda.

And she told Mother all about it.

"Sometimes I feel just like that,"

said Mother.

"Really?" said Amanda.

"Yes," said Mother.

"Everyone has a bad day now and then."

"I'm glad I am here with you

on my bad day," said Amanda.

Mother hugged Amanda some more.

"Are you feeling better yet?" she asked.

"A little," said Amanda. "Keep going."

And they kept on hugging

until the bad sad mad day went away.